SANTA'S
Fun Pack

A GOLDEN BOOK®
Western Publishing Company, Inc.
Racine, Wisconsin 53404

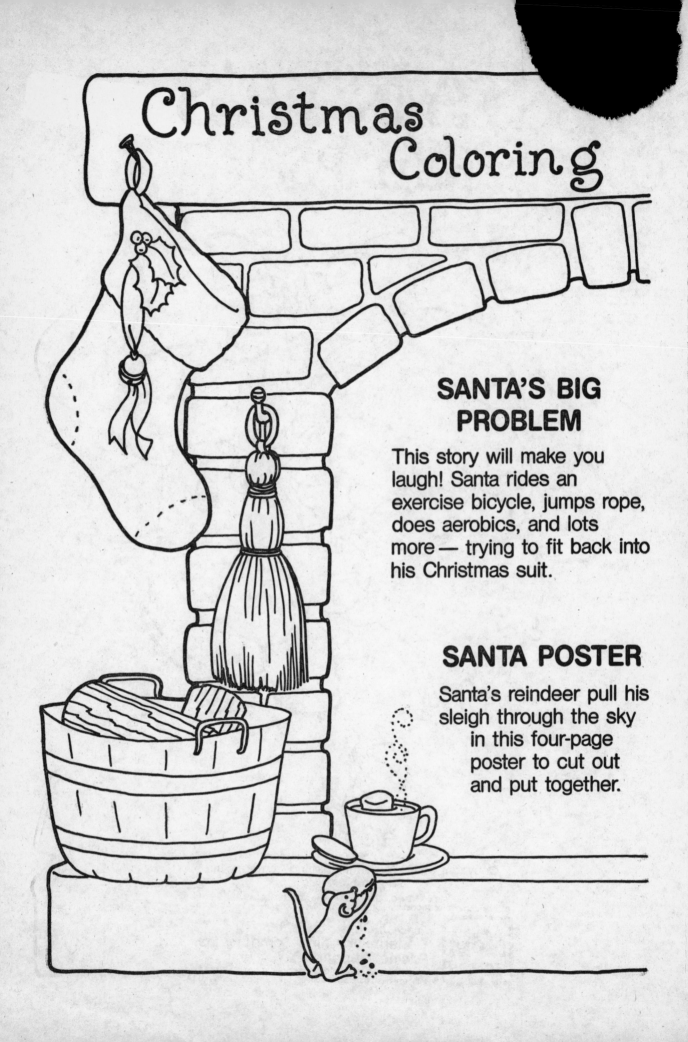

Christmas Coloring

SANTA'S BIG PROBLEM

This story will make you laugh! Santa rides an exercise bicycle, jumps rope, does aerobics, and lots more — trying to fit back into his Christmas suit.

SANTA POSTER

Santa's reindeer pull his sleigh through the sky in this four-page poster to cut out and put together.

and Activity Fun

LOTS OF MAZES
Everything at the North Pole has turned into a maze in this fun-filled section.

HOLIDAY FUN
You'll find hidden pictures, puzzles, games, matchups, and many more things to do.

CHRISTMAS CUTOUTS
Make a holiday door sign, standing Santa, December calendar, and your very own Santa book!

Santa munches cookie after cookie
as he checks the Christmas list.

Mrs. Claus presses Santa's suit . . .

. . . while the elves spruce up his boots and hat.

"OH-OH-OH!" says Santa. "I've been eating
too many cookies. My suit doesn't fit!"

"Bad news," says Mrs. Claus. "I can't make the suit bigger."

"We can't stretch it either," say the elves.

"Maybe I could hold my breath," says Santa.

"Santa, we have a BIG problem," says Eddie Elf.

"What are we going to do?" everyone wonders.

"Christmas is only a few days away!"

The elves come up with a plan.

Mrs. Claus won't let Santa have cookies. . .

. . . or candy . . .

. . . but he can have a *Good-for-You North Pole Frostie!*

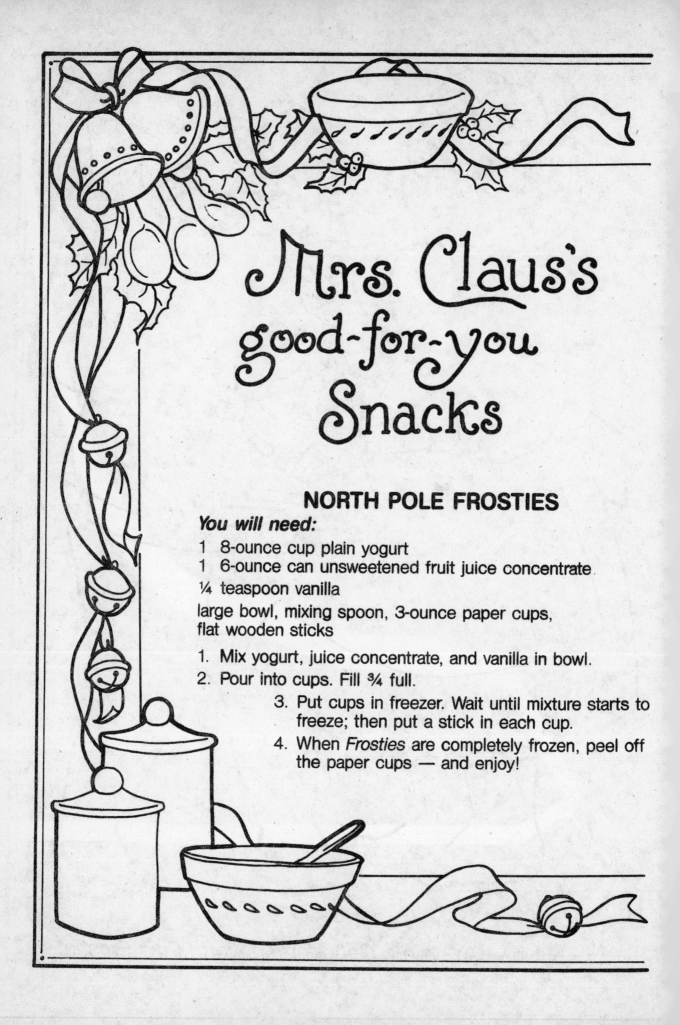

Mrs. Claus's good-for-you Snacks

NORTH POLE FROSTIES

You will need:

1 8-ounce cup plain yogurt
1 6-ounce can unsweetened fruit juice concentrate
¼ teaspoon vanilla

large bowl, mixing spoon, 3-ounce paper cups,
flat wooden sticks

1. Mix yogurt, juice concentrate, and vanilla in bowl.
2. Pour into cups. Fill ¾ full.
3. Put cups in freezer. Wait until mixture starts to freeze; then put a stick in each cup.
4. When *Frosties* are completely frozen, peel off the paper cups — and enjoy!

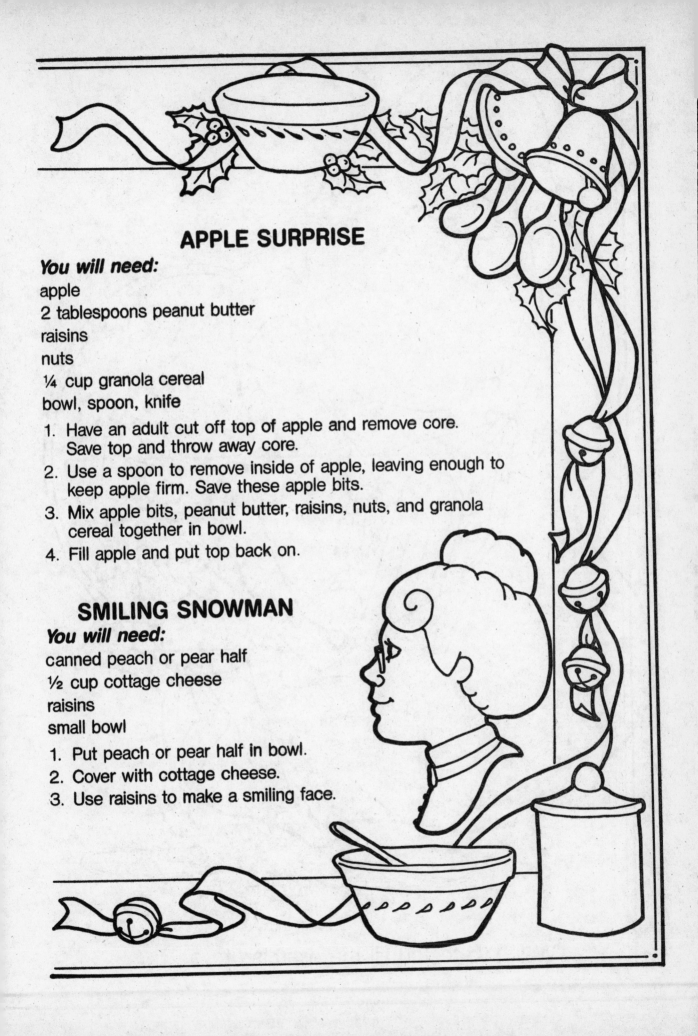

APPLE SURPRISE

You will need:

apple
2 tablespoons peanut butter
raisins
nuts
¼ cup granola cereal
bowl, spoon, knife

1. Have an adult cut off top of apple and remove core. Save top and throw away core.
2. Use a spoon to remove inside of apple, leaving enough to keep apple firm. Save these apple bits.
3. Mix apple bits, peanut butter, raisins, nuts, and granola cereal together in bowl.
4. Fill apple and put top back on.

SMILING SNOWMAN

You will need:

canned peach or pear half
½ cup cottage cheese
raisins
small bowl

1. Put peach or pear half in bowl.
2. Cover with cottage cheese.
3. Use raisins to make a smiling face.

"Well, I've tested all the exercise toys . . . .

. . . and I've eaten lots of healthy snacks,'' says Santa.

"It's Christmas eve," says Mrs. Claus.
"Are you ready to try on your suit?"

Santa's suit fits perfectly!

Merry Christmas

Make a Santa Poster

Directions:

1. Tear out the four poster pages (eight sides).

2. Cut out the poster sections along the outside frame and along the dotted lines.

3. Overlap the sections and tape them so that the frame edges line up.

4. Hang the poster in your room!

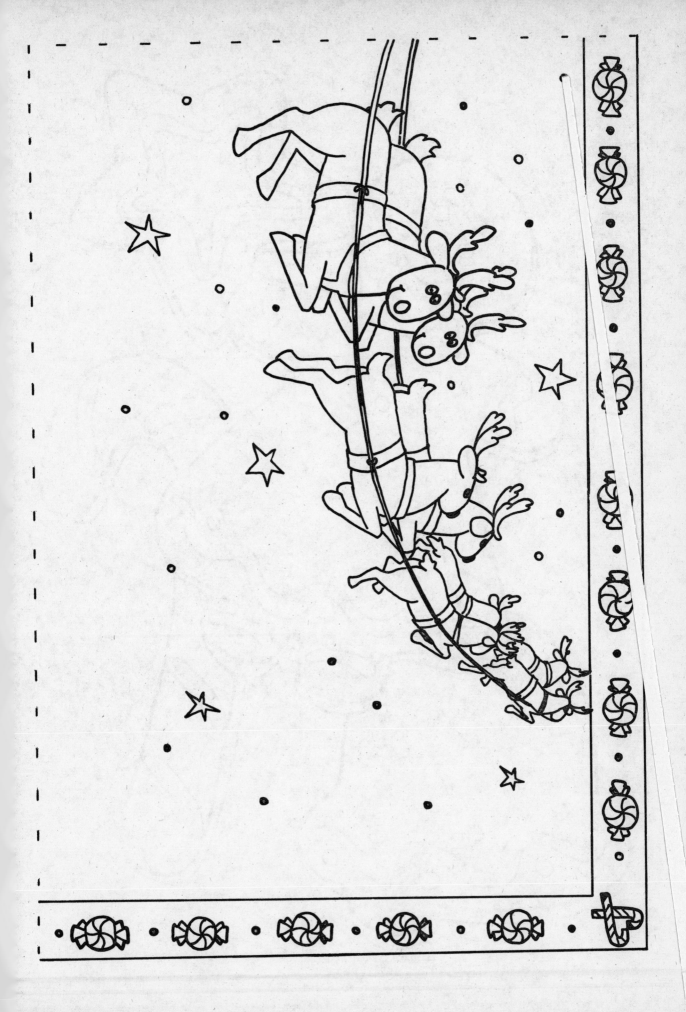

REINDEER HIDE-AND-SEEK. Help Santa find the reindeer that's hiding.

A-MAZ-ING ALPHABET! Help the elf follow the letters of the alphabet in order, so he can get to Santa's workshop.

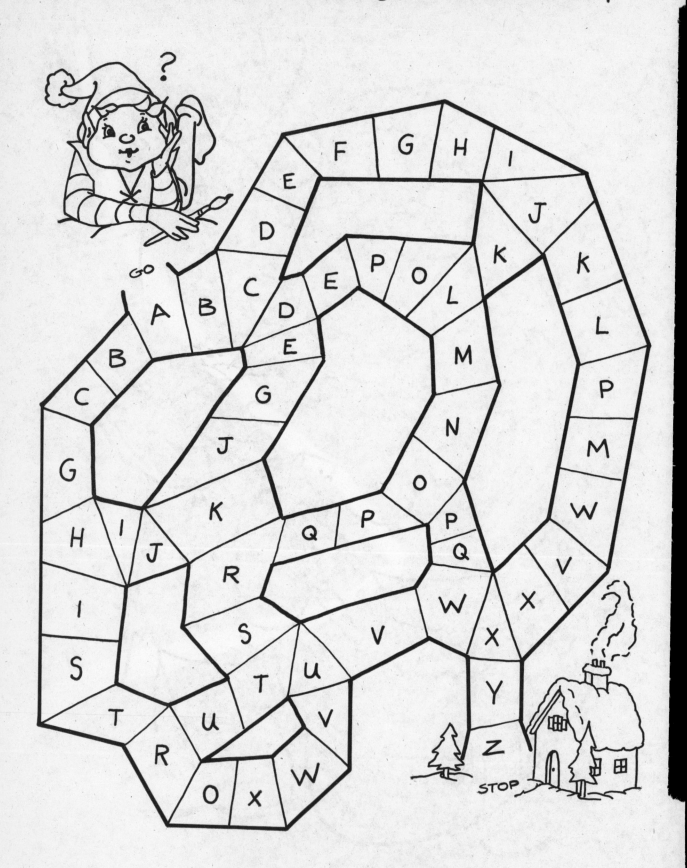

DEAR SANTA! Take the Christmas letter to the North Pole.

CHRISTMAS PETS. Which pet did each child find under the tree?

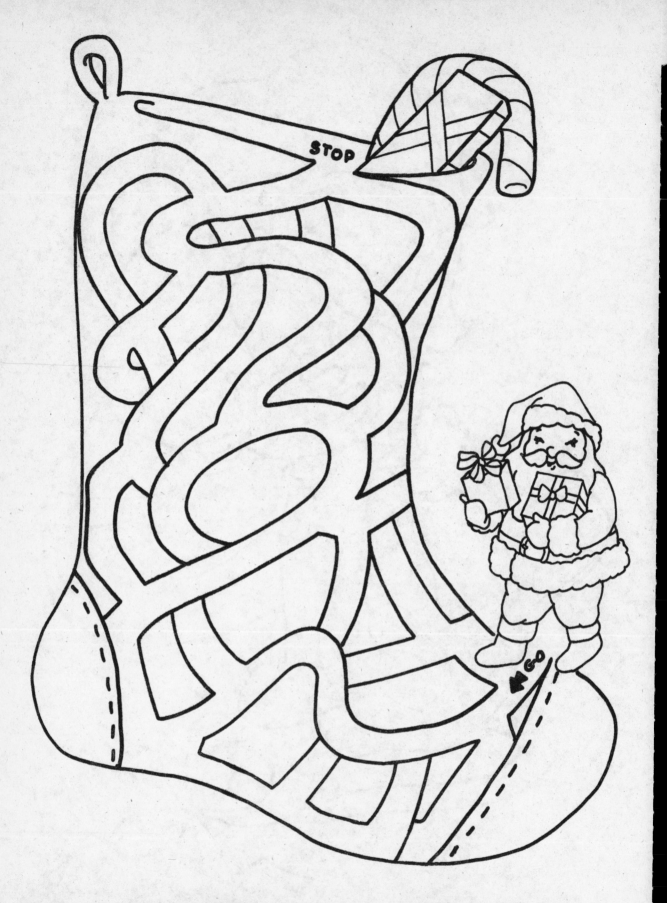

LOTS OF SURPRISES! Help Santa fill the Christmas stocking to the brim!

TOP STAR! Take the tiny elf to the star.

NUMBERS MAZE.
Mrs. Claus wants to share a treat with the elves. To do that, she needs to start at 2 and connect the even numbers in order. Can you help her?

BUSY, BUSY, BUSY! Help each elf find a path to the sleigh without bumping into a buddy.

TREE TIME! These elves want to find the best Christmas tree. To do that, they must follow the one path of trees that add up to 10. Can you find it?

ON, COMET! Which house is next on Santa's list?

RIBBON TANGLE! Which gift belongs to each pet?

CLOUD MAZE. Santa's stuck in the clouds. But some of the clouds are magic! Each magic cloud has a problem that equals 5. Find the magic clouds and draw a path for Santa.

SANTA'S MESSAGE! Help Santa put these toys under the tree. The letters along the correct path spell out a message from Santa. Can you read it?

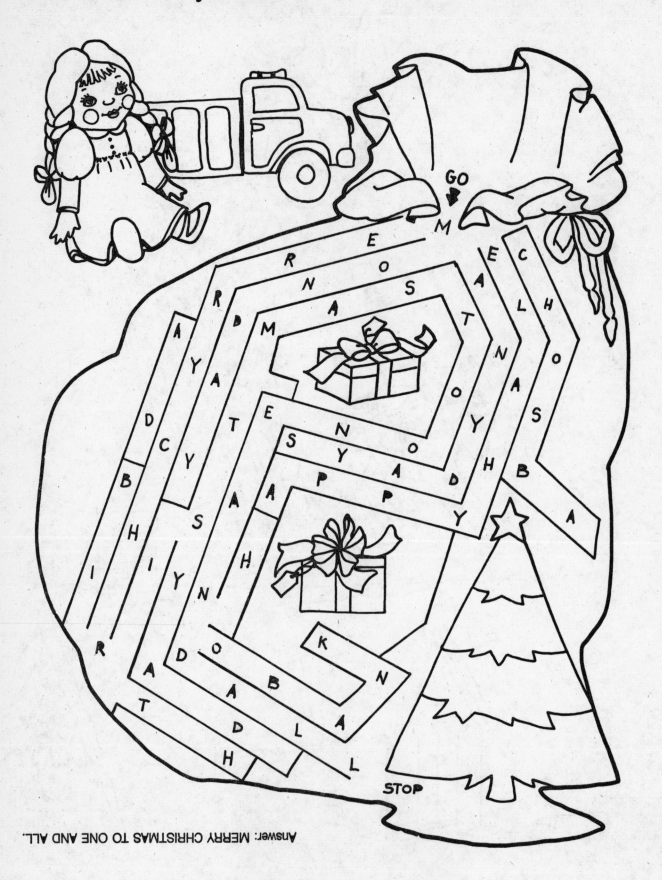

GO

STOP

TEAM UP the reindeer that look alike.

WHAT'S HIDING?

Color the spaces with one dot brown and those with two dots red to find out.

OH-OH!

This letter to Santa fell into a reindeer's food dish and got torn into five pieces. Cut out the pieces and put the letter back together. Rewrite the letter for Santa on the lines on the next page.

_____

_____

_____

_____

_____

_____

_____

_____

_____

_____

Answer:

Dear Santa,
I would like a doll and a puppy for Christmas. My baby brother would like a big red ball.
We will leave a snack on the kitchen table for you and your reindeer. We hope you like it.
Love,
Amy and Scott

FIND THE BROTHERS

Two of the children waiting to see Santa are brothers. To find out who they are, unscramble the letters on the balloons and write the words on the lines. The two boys with words that rhyme are brothers.

_ _ _ _ _

CAROLING PUZZLE

Each clue on the next page describes a letter. Write each letter in the box below that matches its number. One letter is done for you.

Answer: JINGLE BELLS

CLUES:

9. I'm twice in and once in

6. I'm last in and second in

5. I'm once in and twice in

8. I'm twice in and once in

3. I'm third in and last in

10. I'm always in but never in

2. I'm second in and also in

11. I'm fourth in and last in

4. I'm last in and first in

1. I'm first in and first in

7. I'm found in but never in

FIND SANTA'S REINDEER. There are
eight of them hiding in all.

North Pole JUMBLE

Santa can't deliver the toys until he fixes all the jumbled things at the North Pole. Help Santa find five things wrong in this picture.

TAIL MIX-UP

A snowy wind blew through Santa's workshop and mixed up all the tails for toy kittens. Can you help Santa's elf match each tail to its kitten?

TREE TOSS

25

Directions:

Tear out the page. Put a penny on the tree trunk. Take turns with another player flicking the penny onto the decorations. Score the number of points shown on a decoration for landing on it or touching it. Score one point for landing on the tree. The first player to get 150 points wins.

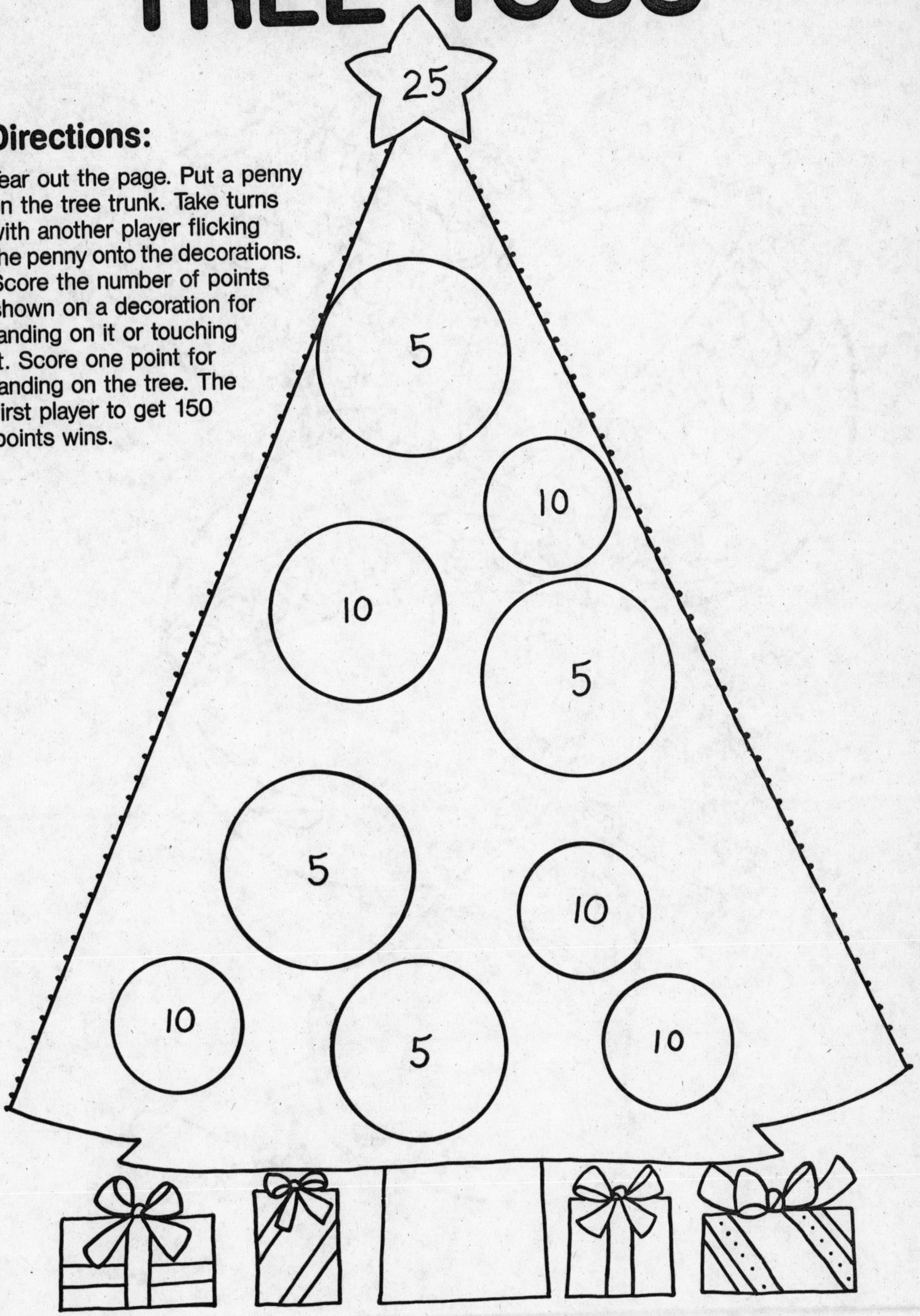

5

10

10

5

5

10

10

5

10

Christmas Crossword. Use the clues to fill in the spaces in the bell.

CLUES:

Across

4. Green and you put lights on it.
6. He says HO-HO-HO.
7. Santa checks this twice.
8. Found under the tree.
9. You string this.
10. White and cold.
13. Santa lives here.
15. Children _ _ _ _ carols.
16. Tree decorations that shine.

Down

1. Santa's reindeer pull this.
2. Red and white candy.
3. Decoration for treetop.
5. Santa's helper.
6. Hangs by fireplace.
11. Decoration often hung on door.
12. Toy for beating.
14. Deck the halls with boughs of _ _ _ _ _.

CHRISTMAS WREATH GAME

Cut out the squares on the next page. Put them in the center of the wreath. Each player chooses a START and marks it with a button. Players take turns tossing a penny. Move 2 spaces in the direction of the arrows for heads; move 1 space for tails. Each player takes as many squares from the center of the wreath as it says on the space where he/she lands. A player landing on a candy cane gets 5 squares; a player landing on a jack-o'-lantern loses 5 squares. Players keep going around until all the squares are gone. The player with the most squares wins!

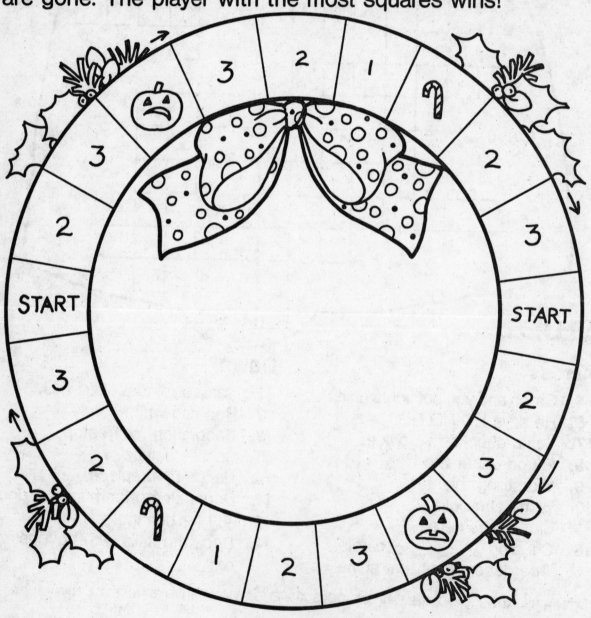

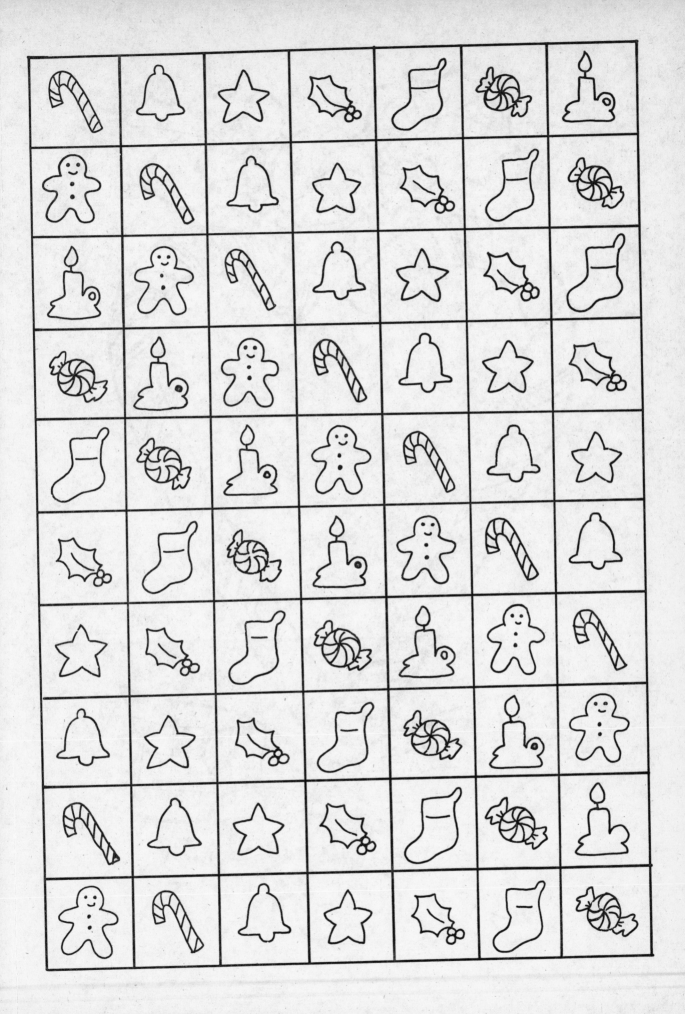

Decorate the Christmas cookies.

WHAT'S WRONG with the toys? One night the elves worked until they were very sleepy. They made mistakes on all of the toys in this picture. Can you find what's wrong so the elves can fix the toys?

WHO DID IT?

One of Santa's elves painted the sleigh bright and shiny. Santa wants to thank the elf, but he doesn't know which one did it. Be a detective and use the clues to help Santa find out who the painter is.

Clues:

1. The painter has a buckle on his hat. Draw a line through everyone who does not have a buckle on his hat.

2. The painter doesn't have a mustache. Draw a line through everyone who has a mustache.

3. The painter has a paint smudge on his face. Draw a line through everyone who does not have a paint smudge on his face.

4. The painter is wearing striped leggings. Draw a line through everyone who is not wearing striped leggings.

5. The painter has bells on the toes of his shoes. Draw a line through everyone who does not have bells on the toes of his shoes.

5.

6.

7.

8.

9.

10.

Now that you've used all the clues, there should only be one elf without a line through him. That's the painter elf Santa wants to thank.

FIND THE TREATS
Mrs. Claus has hidden in the workshop to surprise the elves. Look closely to see: gingerbread man, candy cane, pitcher of hot chocolate, Christmas cake, plate of cookies, jar of candy, gingerbread house.

MY STARS!

Santa's elf is having fun counting the triangles in this Christmas star. How many can you find?

HELP SANTA fill this stocking. Look up, down, forward, and backward to find the *stocking stuffers* in the block of letters.

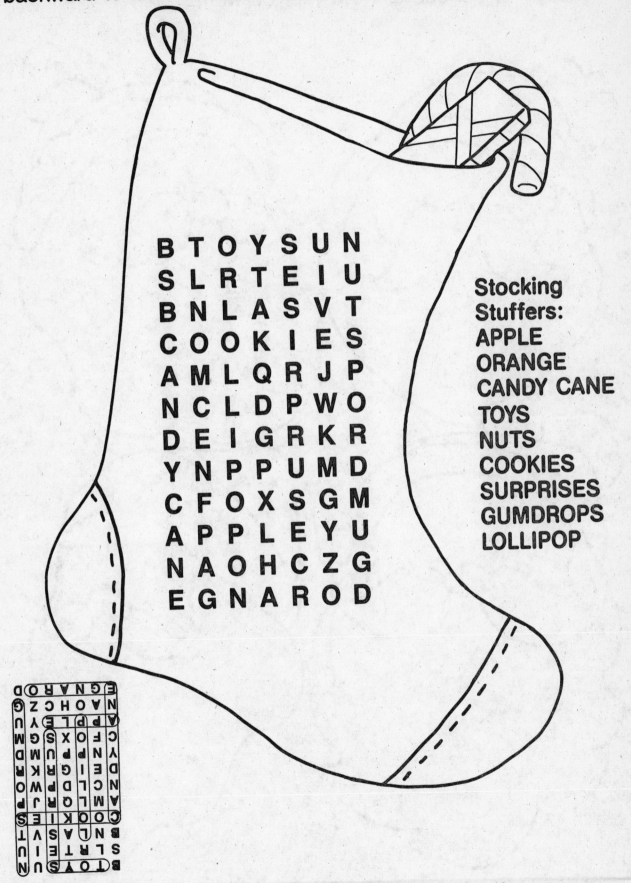

```
B T O Y S U N
S L R T E I U
B N L A S V T
C O O K I E S
A M L Q R J P
N C L D P W O
D E I G R K R
Y N P P U M D
C F O X S G M
A P P L E Y U
N A O H C Z G
E G N A R O D
```

Stocking Stuffers:
APPLE
ORANGE
CANDY CANE
TOYS
NUTS
COOKIES
SURPRISES
GUMDROPS
LOLLIPOP

Finish the **SANTA FACES.** Make Santa look happy or serious or however you want.

WHO'S PEEKING IN?

Cut out the strip of faces on the next page. Also cut slits on the dotted lines of the window. Thread the strip through the slits to see who's watching Santa and the elves at work.

Jolly Standing Santa

1. Cut out Santa and tab along dotted lines. (Be sure to cut under Santa's arms.)
2. Cut out slot.
3. Put tab through slot.
4. Stand your Santa up.

TAB

Make Your Own
DECEMBER
CALENDAR

1. Tear out these two pages.
2. Cut out the Santa scene and tape it to top of calendar.
3. Fill in the dates on calendar.
4. Cut out the labels and paste them on calendar. Write your own things to do on the blank labels.
5. Hang the calendar in your room.

Trim Tree

Hang Stocking

Wrap Gifts

Help Bake

Write Christmas List

Visit a Friend

Go Caroling

Make Christmas Cards

December

SUNDAY	MONDAY	TUESDAY	WEDNESDAY	THURSDAY	FRIDAY	SATURDAY

Directions:

Tear out the page.

Cut out book pages 1, 3, and 5 along the dotted lines.

Put page 1 on top of page 3, and page 3 on top of page 5.

Staple the pages together along the left edge.

My Santa Book

1

3

5